Ladybird books are widely available, but in case of
difficulty may be ordered by post or telephone from:

Ladybird Books – Cash Sales Department
Littlegate Road Paignton Devon TQ3 3BE
Telephone 01803 554761

A catalogue record for this book is available
from the British Library

Published by Ladybird Books Ltd Loughborough Leicestershire UK
LADYBIRD and the device of a Ladybird are trademarks of Ladybird Books Ltd

Britt Allcroft's Magic Adventures of Mumfie
Created by Britt Allcroft from the works of Katharine Tozer
Written by Britt Allcroft and John Kane
Song lyrics by John Kane
© Britt Allcroft (Mumfie) Ltd MCMXCV
All rights worldwide Britt Allcroft (Mumfie) Ltd
MUMFIE is a trademark of Britt Allcroft (Mumfie) Ltd
The BRITT ALLCROFT logo is a trademark of The Britt Allcroft Group Ltd

Britt Allcroft's Magic Adventures of Mumfie

Pirates Ahoy!

Ladybird

The story so far…

Mumfie, the special little elephant, was looking for an exciting adventure.

He had found an enchanted island belonging to the Queen of Night. But the Queen's wicked Secretary had stolen her magic and turned the island into a prison.

Mumfie, and his new friends, Scarecrow, Pinkey, Whale and Napoleon, were determined to free Pinkey's mother, who was imprisoned on the island, and help the Queen of Night.

While on the island, Mumfie had accidentally found the Queen's wonderful jewel and then  lost it in the ocean! The Secretary needed this jewel to make his magic complete.

Then, during a pirate attack, Mumfie and Scarecrow had become separated from Whale and Pinkey.

Mumfie and Scarecrow spent the night in Mrs Admiral's house on the seabed. Mrs Admiral's husband had been captured by the pirates. Mumfie promised to look for him as well as for Whale, Pinkey and the Queen's jewel…

Mumfie and Scarecrow set off the next day to begin their search for Whale, Pinkey and Mr Admiral.

Mrs Admiral packed the two friends a big picnic basket and waved goodbye from her little cottage.

"Thank you for mending my coat," called Mumfie.

"Davy Jones, the captain of them pirates," warned Mrs Admiral, "is a dark and dangerous man, so be on your guard at *all* times."

Mumfie and Scarecrow searched all morning. They found many strange and wonderful things but there was no sign of Whale, Pinkey or Mr Admiral. At last, they came to a big cave.

"If I was a pirate, that's just the sort of place I'd store my treasure," said Mumfie.

So, trying to feel brave, Mumfie and Scarecrow stepped carefully into the shadows of the mysterious cave. It was very dark inside and the ground was wet and slimy. Suddenly, Mumfie slipped and lost his balance. He grabbed Scarecrow and they both slid down a steep slope.

When Mumfie finally reached the bottom, he realised that Scarecrow wasn't with him. He began to feel afraid. "*Please* say something, Scarecrow," called Mumfie.

Suddenly, Mumfie saw a dazzling light above him — it was an electric eel.

"You're very bright," said Mumfie.

"I always was, even as a child," replied the eel. "Wait a bit and I'll turn myself down."

The eel looked friendly enough so Mumfie told her all about Scarecrow.

"I've seen him!" cried Eel. "Follow me." And in no time at all, Mumfie and Scarecrow were reunited.

"Now, back to business," said Mumfie to Eel. "We're looking for pirates. Can you help us find them?"

Eel shuddered.

"Pirates have a nasty habit of sticking us electric eels in jam jars just to light up their parties," Eel said.

"But we're trying to find Mr Admiral," explained Mumfie. "We're afraid the pirates may have captured him."

When Eel heard this, she became very angry. "This way!" she cried, and set off at a crackling pace. Mumfie and Scarecrow hurried after her.

At last, Eel stopped. Below them, in the middle of a seaweed forest, lay the pirate ship, *Sea Witch*. They could hear the pirates singing.

"Now you can see what you're up against," said Eel.

"Yes, indeed," said Mumfie. "But I'm sure we'll find the Admiral in that pirate ship, so we have to go there."

He's not a Whatifer, Scarecrow thought to himself. That was one of the things Scarecrow liked best about Mumfie.

Whatifer was Scarecrow's name for people who would say things like, "What if he's not on board the ship?" or "What if we are captured by pirates?" Deep down, Scarecrow thought he was a Whatifer himself, but he decided to follow Mumfie anyway.

As Mumfie and Scarecrow began to silently climb the ship's ladder, the little elephant asked Eel to look for Whale and Pinkey, and to make sure they were safe. Without another word, Eel was gone.

Halfway up the ladder, Mumfie spotted someone through a porthole. "He looks just like the man in Mrs Admiral's photo!" he gasped. "We've *found* the Admiral!"

"And what do you think *you're* doing?" said a nasty one-eyed pirate, glaring down at Mumfie and Scarecrow. He ordered the two friends onto the deck.

There, waiting for them, was the pirate captain, Davy Jones.

"My name is Mumfie," said the little elephant, "and this is Scarecrow. We're looking for the Admiral."

"And I'm the dangerous Davy Jones," snarled the Captain. Then, pointing to a pirate called Nasty Nate he said, "Take these scurvy swabs to the laundry room. They're all washed up, just like the Admiral!"

Meanwhile, Eel had found Whale. He was tied with nets and strong, steel rope to the bottom of the seabed. Pinkey was gazing anxiously through one of Whale's portholes.

"It's those pesky pirates," Eel said. "And by the look of it, they've certainly been up to their old tricks again."

Whale looked very miserable.

"Don't worry," said Eel. "I think I can get you out of this mess. I'll be back in a flash." And she darted off.

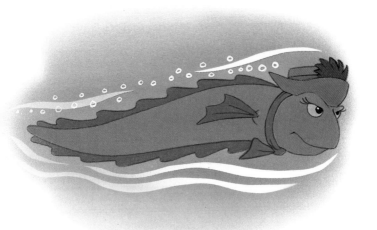

Eel soon returned with a group of her friends. "If we make enough sparks," she explained to Whale, "we'll be able to cut through the ropes and free you."

The electric eels set to work and, at last, Whale swam free.

"You'd better swim to the surface, Whale," advised Eel. "You'll be a lot safer there."

"Thank you very much," boomed Whale, "but I'm not going anywhere. Mumfie and Scarecrow may need me here."

"I'll find out," replied Eel. And with Pinkey safely tucked under her hat, she whizzed away as fast as she could back towards the pirate ship.

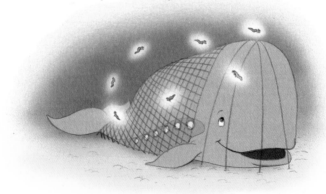

On board the pirate's ship, in the captain's cabin, Davy Jones was peering through his periscope. Suddenly, he noticed the wicked Secretary flying towards him.

"Captain Jones," hissed the Secretary. "I have need of your services. If you can find the Queen's jewel and bring it to me, *I* shall rule the land and *you* can rule the seas."

It was an offer Davy Jones couldn't refuse and he immediately began his search.

Below deck, in the laundry room, Mumfie, Scarecrow and the Admiral were trying to think of a way to escape.

Suddenly, Eel and Pinkey appeared through the porthole. This gave Mumfie an idea for getting a message to their friend Napoleon, back in the Queen's palace – a message in a bottle!

"But it could be years before the bottle is washed up anywhere," said the Admiral.

"Not if Eel guided it to the beach," suggested Scarecrow.

"What a good idea!" cried Mumfie. "And then Pinkey can fly on to find Napoleon."

Soon, the message was ready:

Dear Napoleon,

We have been captured by underwater pirates. Here is a map of our whereabouts. Anything you can do to help would be much appreciated.

Hope you are well!

Kindest regards,
Mumfie, Scarecrow and the Admiral.

The Admiral put the message into a bottle.

Then, with Pinkey safely tucked under her hat, Eel took the bottle in her mouth. With a last wave of her tail, Eel was gone. She wriggled up towards the surface and headed for the mysterious island.

Mumfie, Scarecrow and the Admiral, left all alone again, began making further plans for escape…

They decided to disguise Mumfie and Scarecrow as one tall pirate. Mumfie sat on Scarecrow's shoulders and the Admiral buttoned a big coat around them.

"Who are *you?*" said Nasty Nate, coming in with some washing.

"I'm a new crew member," said Mumfie, trying to sound fierce, "with orders to give the prisoner some exercise on deck."

So, Nasty Nate led Mumfie, Scarecrow and the Admiral up onto the ship's deck. "We're out," whispered Mumfie to Scarecrow.

Suddenly, they heard a gruff voice behind them. "Who's *this* wearing *my* coat?" growled Davy Jones. "Take it off—*now!*"

Unfortunately, Mumfie and Scarecrow had put on the Captain's favourite outfit!

Scarecrow began to unbutton the coat. As he did so, Mumfie glimpsed something bright and shining in Davy Jones' pocket. "The Queen's jewel!" he said softly to his friends. "The Captain's found the Queen's jewel."

As Scarecrow took the coat off, Davy Jones roared, "It's them stowaways!" and lunged at Mumfie.

But the Admiral was too quick for Davy Jones and threw a bucket of soapy water at him. The pirate captain slipped, and the jewel fell out of his pocket – Mumfie grabbed it!

"I've got it!" shouted Mumfie.

"Run for it!" cried the Admiral.

The three friends ran to the edge of the ship and climbed over the side.

"After them!" screamed Davy Jones at the other pirates. So the *Sea Witch* set sail and began to follow them...

Far away, Pinkey and Eel had reached the mysterious island. Pinkey took the message from the bottle and flew on to look for Napoleon. Eel swam back to the pirate ship to help Mumfie.

Eventually, after a long and tiring search, Pinkey found Napoleon just as Bristle, the prison guard, was approaching.

"Can you fly?" cried Pinkey.

Napoleon looked unsure. "I had my wings clipped long ago," he sighed.

"Well, perhaps they've grown back again," Pinkey encouraged.

Napoleon stretched out one wing and then the other. They worked perfectly! The next moment he and Pinkey were soaring into the sky in search of Whale and their other friends – Bristle was left *far* behind!

Below the sea, Mumfie, Scarecrow and the Admiral were still being chased by the pirate ship through the seaweed forest.

Suddenly, the net that had once held Whale to the seabed fell over the ship. The pirates were trapped! Mumfie and the Admiral looked up in surprise and saw Eel. She and all of her helpers quickly secured the net in place.

"Well done, ladies," boomed a deep voice – it was Whale! And there, looking through his portholes were Pinkey, Napoleon and Mrs Admiral.

"Climb aboard, my friends!" continued Whale, who was delighted to see Mumfie and the others again.

As the friends told of their adventures, Whale set to work tightening the ropes around the pirate ship.

Everyone was so busy that no one saw Davy Jones slip away.

The Admiral and Mrs Admiral were so pleased to see each other again that they couldn't say a word and hugged each other all the way home.

When Whale reached the Admiral's house, Mumfie and his friends said goodbye to them.

"I'm sorry we have to go," said Mumfie, "but we still have *very* important work to do on the island. There's no time to lose!"

Above them, they could hear the rumble of thunder and the crash of lightning...

The storm clouds are gathering! Mumfie can tell that the wicked Secretary is angry. But now that all his friends are together again, he knows he has the power to defeat the Secretary once and for all...

Friendship is a circle that grows
wider every day,
Throw a pebble in the water,
see the circles grow.
Day by day the heart becomes
more fond,
When the rain is falling,
see the circles that it makes.
Round and round the feeling goes,
friendship is a circle,
On and on forever,
friendship is a circle
That never will close.

But how Mumfie and his friends rescue the island from the wicked Secretary will have to wait until the next time!

Book four: **A Treasure Beyond Price.**